In memory of Grandma Mollie

Thanks to Stephanie Rayner, my instructor at The Haliburton School of The Arts, who taught me the technique of watercolor monoprint. Thanks also to Sue Tate, Elizabeth Kribs, Five Seventeen, Sylvia Chan and Tara Walker of Tundra Books and Chris Barash and Geoff Oldmixon of PJ Library, who all played a role in the making of this book.

Library and Archives Canada Cataloguing in Publication

Ungar, Richard, author
Yitzi and the giant menorah / Richard Ungar.

Issued in print and electronic formats.
ISBN 978-1-77049-812-9 (bound)
ISBN 978-1-77049-814-3 (epub)

I. Title.

PS8591.N42Y57 2016   jC813'.6   C2015-906953-X
C2015-906954-8

Published simultaneously in the United States of America by Tundra Books of Northern New York, a division of Random House of Canada Limited, a Penguin Random House Company

Library of Congress Control Number: 2015955121

Edited by Sue Tate

The illustrations in this book are watercolor monoprints.
Please visit www.richard-ungar.com to see how they were made.

The text was set in LTC Powell and Celestia Antiqua.

Printed and bound in China

www.penguinrandomhouse.ca

1 2 3 4 5   20 19 18 17 16

Yitzi and the Giant Menorah

by **Richard Ungar**

TUNDRA BOOKS

One cold morning, on the eve of Hanukkah,
a wagon rolled into Chelm.

"People of Chelm," the wagon driver announced, "the
Mayor of Lublin wishes to bestow upon you a special gift."

Huddling together to stay warm, the villagers all
tried to guess what the special gift might be.

"A fine cedar bench for the synagogue," said Avrum
the Carpenter.

"A golden water pump," said Hayim the
Water Carrier.

"An oceanful of herring!" said Shmulik the
Herring Vendor.

The villagers held their breath as the wagon driver flung blankets from a huge object strapped to the wagon.

"Yitzi," whispered Avrum to his son, "I have never seen a tree as beautiful as that one."

"It is not a tree, Father. It's . . . a menorah!" Yitzi watched in amazement as the wagon driver, with help from the villagers, unloaded the biggest menorah he had ever seen. Eight dazzling branches flowed from a magnificent stem.

That evening, all the villagers met in the square to watch the lighting of the giant menorah for the first night of Hanukkah.

"Fellow Chelmites," said Avrum. "We must find a way to thank the Mayor of Lublin for this wonderful gift."

Everyone nodded. Such a gift was surely deserving of more than a simple thank-you.

Later, as they returned to their homes, each villager pondered the same question: *What is the most fitting way to thank the Mayor of Lublin?*

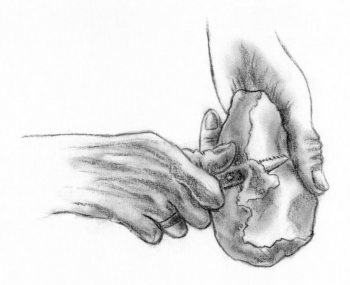

On the second night of Hanukkah, after the giant menorah had been lit, Rivka the Cook declared, "I have it! I will make the mayor a special batch of my famous potato latkes."

"An excellent idea!" the villagers agreed.

The sun had barely risen the next morning when Rivka began cooking her famous latkes. As soon as they were ready, she wrapped them up and handed the bundle to Shmulik.

"Ride like the wind, Shmulik. You must get to Lublin before the latkes cool down. And here," said Rivka, "take this jug of applesauce to go with them."

Shmulik hopped on his horse, Lucille, and began the journey to Lublin. Before long, the aroma of latkes made Shmulik dizzy with desire. He could stand it no longer. Ripping open the bundle, he devoured all of the latkes in less than a minute. And while Shmulik was eating the latkes, Lucille slurped all of the applesauce.

When they saw what they had done, Shmulik and Lucille hung their heads low, turned around and headed back to Chelm.

On the third night of Hanukkah, after the giant menorah had been lit, Yitzi turned to Avrum. "Father, we still haven't sung any Hanukkah songs!"

"There is no time for singing, Yitzi!" answered Avrum. "We must solve the problem of how to thank the Mayor of Lublin."

"Listen up, everyone," said Hayim the next morning. "I have it! The best way to thank the mayor is to give him something he can't possibly find in Lublin."

"But, Hayim," said Avrum, "what does Chelm have that Lublin does not?"

"The answer lies all around us," said Hayim.

"All I see is snow," said Avrum.

"Precisely," said Hayim.

"But, Hayim, Lublin has snow too," said Shmulik.

"Of course. But our snow is whiter and much more sparkly!"

Hayim loaded up his cart with two big barrelfuls of special Chelm snow and set out for Lublin. The sun shone brightly as the cart bounced along. Soon it was so warm that Hayim had to undo the buttons on his coat. When he glanced back to check on the barrels, he received a terrible shock. All of the snow had disappeared, and the barrels held only water!

"Wait until I catch the thief who stole my snow," Hayim grumbled. Then he turned his cart around and headed back to Chelm.

On the fourth night of Hanukkah, after the giant menorah had been lit, Yitzi said, "Father, can we sing at least one Hanukkah song tonight?"

"Yitzi, we have more pressing business than singing songs," answered Avrum. Then, turning to everyone, he said, "I have it! I will carve a fine dreidel for the mayor. Whenever he spins it, he will think of Chelm."

Avrum hurried to his shop and worked late into the night. In the morning, he showed everyone the dreidel he had carved.

"Exquisite!" they all agreed.

So Avrum hitched his horse to his wagon and set off for Lublin. On the way, he couldn't resist stopping to spin the dreidel.

The hoot of an owl brought Avrum to his senses. *Oh no! Where has the day gone? I must hurry to Lublin . . . but which way is it?* He looked up and down the road. *I know, I will spin the dreidel one more time. Whichever direction it points must surely be the right way.*

Whistling to himself, Avrum spun the dreidel and set off in the direction it pointed. He soon found himself in Minsk. When he spun the dreidel again, he ended up in Warsaw! By the time Avrum arrived back in Chelm (without ever finding his way to Lublin), the fifth and sixth nights of Hanukkah had already come and gone.

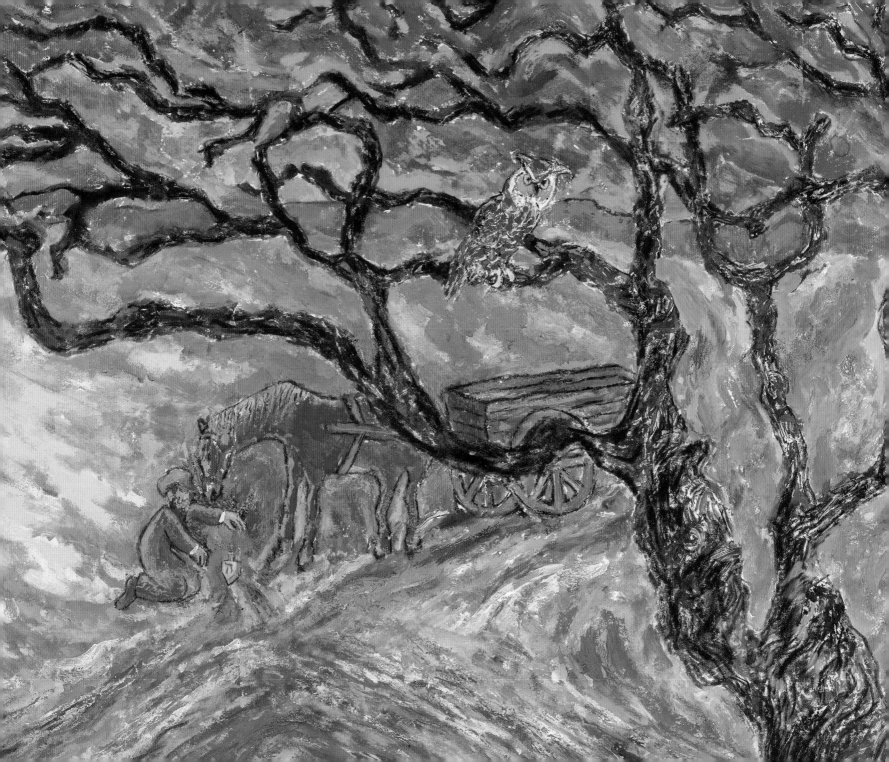

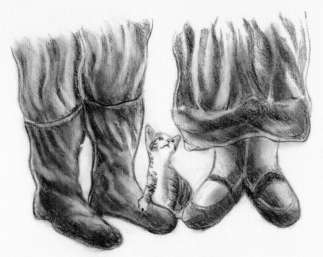

On the seventh evening, after the giant menorah had been lit, the villagers gathered in the town hall.

"People of Chelm," Avrum announced, "tomorrow night is the last night of Hanukkah. If we do not thank the Mayor of Lublin by then, he will most certainly think us ungrateful."

A small voice piped up, "I have an idea, Father."

"Yitzi," said Avrum impatiently, "now is not the time for singing!"

"Everyone, please listen!" said Yitzi. "Shmulik, you must ride to Lublin and ask the mayor to climb the big hill outside of town tomorrow evening."

"And what is the gift I should bring?" said Shmulik.

"There is no need for you to bring anything," said Yitzi.

"But surely I must bring a gift with me to thank the mayor?"

"Trust me," said Yitzi. "The mayor will find his gift when he gets to the top of the hill."

The following day, when the sun was high, everyone met in the village square. At Yitzi's urging, they lifted the giant menorah onto a cart and set out for the hill just outside of Chelm.

It was slow going, slogging up the big hill. By the time they finally reached the top, the sun had already set. And no sooner had they put it down than it was time to light the giant menorah for the last night of Hanukkah.

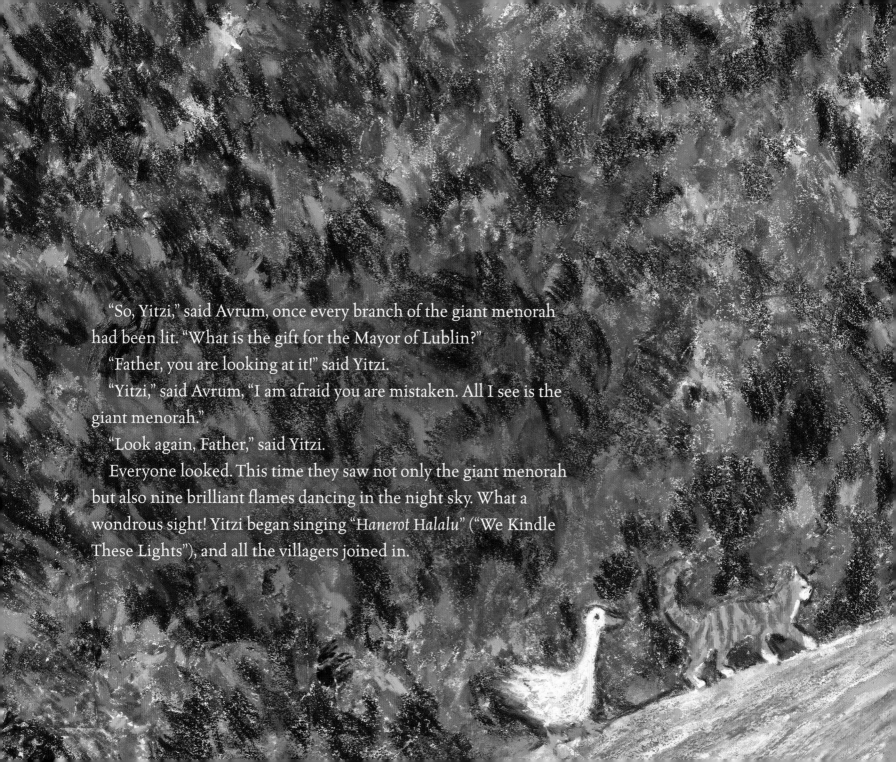

"So, Yitzi," said Avrum, once every branch of the giant menorah had been lit. "What is the gift for the Mayor of Lublin?"

"Father, you are looking at it!" said Yitzi.

"Yitzi," said Avrum, "I am afraid you are mistaken. All I see is the giant menorah."

"Look again, Father," said Yitzi.

Everyone looked. This time they saw not only the giant menorah but also nine brilliant flames dancing in the night sky. What a wondrous sight! Yitzi began singing "*Hanerot Halalu*" ("We Kindle These Lights"), and all the villagers joined in.

At that very moment, under the same night sky, the mayor trudged up the hill outside of Lublin. It was a long climb, and his legs felt heavier with every step. After a while, he had to stop. "I am too tired to carry on," he said to himself.

Just then he heard a sound. It was only a faint wisp carried by the wind, but it sounded like singing. With renewed strength, he began to climb again. Finally arriving at the top of the hill, he turned toward the direction of the music. Something on a distant hill filled his heart with joy.

It was the giant menorah, lit up in all its magnificence.

The Mayor of Lublin stood there for a long time, delighting in the perfect thank-you from Yitzi and the people of Chelm.

The Story of Chanukah*

The story of Chanukah happened a long, long time ago in the land of Israel. At that time, the Holy Temple in Jerusalem was the most special place for the Jewish people. The Temple contained many beautiful objects, including a tall, golden menorah. Unlike menorahs of today, this menorah had seven (rather than nine) branches and was lit not by candles or light bulbs, but by oil. Every evening, oil would be poured into the cups that sat on top of the menorah. The Temple would glow with shimmering light.

At the time of the Chanukah story, a cruel king named Antiochus ruled over the land of Israel. "I don't like the Jewish people," declared Antiochus. "They are so different from me. I don't celebrate Shabbat or read from the Torah, so why should they?" Antiochus ordered the Jewish people to stop being Jewish and to pray to Greek gods. "No more going to the Temple, no more celebrating Shabbat and no more Torah!" shouted Antiochus. He sent his guards to ransack the Temple. They brought mud and garbage into the Temple. They broke furniture, tore curtains and smashed the jars of oil that were used to light the menorah.

This made the Jews very angry. One Jew named Judah Maccabee cried out, "We must stop Antiochus! We must think of ways to make him leave the land of Israel." At first, Judah's followers, called the Maccabees, were afraid. "Judah," they said, "Antiochus has so many soldiers. They carry big weapons and wear armor. He even uses elephants to fight his battles. How can we Jews, who don't have weapons, fight against him?" Judah replied, "If we think very hard and plan very carefully, we will be able to defeat him." It took a long time, but at last the Maccabees chased Antiochus and his men out of Israel.

As soon as Antiochus and his soldiers were gone, the Jewish people hurried to Jerusalem to clean their Temple. What a mess! The beautiful menorah was gone, and the floor was covered with trash, broken furniture and jagged pieces from the shattered jars of oil. The Maccabees built a new menorah. At first they worried that they would not be able to light their new menorah, but they searched and searched, until at last they found one tiny jar of oil – enough to light the menorah for just one evening. The Maccabees knew that it would be at least eight days until they could get more oil, but they lit the menorah anyway. To their surprise, this little jar of oil burned for eight days. The Jewish people could not believe their good fortune. First, their small army had chased away Antiochus' large army, and now the tiny jar of oil had lasted for eight whole days!

The Jewish people prayed and thanked God for these miracles. Every year during Chanukah, Jews light menorahs for eight days to remember the miracles that happened long ago.

* The transliterated word Chanukah can be spelled in a number of different ways – including Hanukkah, Chanuka, etc.